Adventures of Mac the Dog

MW00986844

By: Tamara Cantarano

Illustrations by Anita Waller

For Devin~My sillybug that started me all over again.
And always makes me smile. T.C.

For all my girls~Whether two or four legged. Past present
and future, you are my world. A.W.

This is a story about a puppy dog named Mac.
He is a happy dog.

One day Mac heard the circus was coming to his neighborhood in New York!

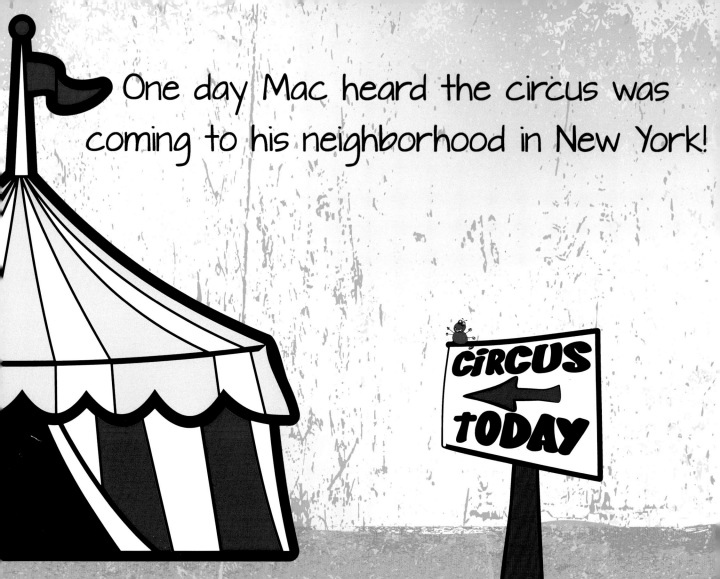

CiRCUS
TODAY

This news made him very excited.

One of his dreams
was to see the circus!

He ran all the way there.

When he got there a sign read "No pets allowed".

Mac was sad... but he had an idea!
He was not just a pet.
Maybe he could be a circus animal?

He thought he'd enter with the elephants,

but he didn't look like an elephant.

He was going to go in with a bearded lady,

but he knew better than to go with a stranger.

Mac wondered if he could help the lions with their tricks,

but that would be too dangerous.

He sniffed out a pile of colorful clothing.

He tried them on and had the best idea yet.

Dressed as a clown,
    he was allowed right in.

He was happy!
    He was silly!

He was bouncy!

He made everyone smile.

Mac enjoyed being at the circus and IN the circus. What really made him feel good was making people happy and seeing them smile.